Princess Kira's
Kiwi Jubilee

Princess Kira's
Kiwi Jubilee

Sudipta Bardhan-Quallen

AMULET BOOKS • NEW YORK

Cataloging-in-Publication Data has been applied for and may be obtained from the Library of Congress.

ISBN 978-1-4197-6638-1

PRINCESS POWER™/© Netflix. Used with permission.
Based on *Princesses Wear Pants* created by
Savannah Guthrie and Allison Oppenheim
Interior illustrations by Thais Bolton
Book design by Brann Garvey and Becky James

Printed and bound in U.S.A.
10 9 8 7 6 5 4 3 2 1

Amulet Books are available at special discounts when purchased in quantity for premiums and promotions as well as fundraising or educational use. Special editions can also be created to specification. For details, contact specialsales@abramsbooks.com or the address below.

ABRAMS The Art of Books
195 Broadway, New York, NY 10007
abramsbooks.com

To Princess Anika and Princess Roxie
—S.B.Q.

Meet the princesses

Kira Kiwi

An animal expert with a caring heart, Kira never met a creature who she didn't love.

Penny Pineapple

With a curious mind and her love of science, Penny can solve big problems in a pinch.

of the Four Fruitdoms!

Rita Raspberry

As the kingdoms' resident artist, Rita always brings some razzle-dazzle to every situation.

Bea Blueberry

A confident and fearless athlete, Bea says what she thinks and never hesitates to jump into action.

Chapter 1

Princess Kira was always ready to help the fruitizens of the Kiwi Fruitdom. "Everyone deserves Kiwi kindness," she said. And she meant *everyone*—the people in the kingdom and the animals, too!

The Kiwi Jubilee was a celebration of Kiwi kindness. Anyone from any of the four Fruitdoms could come. It was Kira's favorite party of the year!

"We're almost ready for tonight," said Kira's mother, Queen Katia. "Kira and Karina, can you help me clean up the garden?" Karina was Kira's big sister.

"Mr. Scrumples and I are here to help!" Kira said, scooping up her hamster.

Outside the palace, Queen Katia sent Karina to sweep the gazebo. Then she said, "Kira, could you double-check the garden? I don't want any trash left out accidentally."

Wild teenykins would often visit the royal garden. Kira knew it was important

to always keep the garden clean so that no teenykin got hurt. "We're expert garden cleaners!" she exclaimed.

Kira and Mr. Scrumples checked bushes, flower beds, and benches.

In no time at all, they had inspected most of the garden. "There's only one place left to double-check," Kira said. She pointed. "The gazebo! I'll race you, Mr. Scrumples!"

They both scampered off toward the gazebo. Kira's legs were longer, though, so she moved faster. She was about to win when she saw something and slowed down. *What's that?* she wondered.

A bit of white fuzz was tucked under the gazebo. Was it trash? Kira bent down to get a closer look. Mr. Scrumples raced past her, right to the gazebo. Then he did a little victory dance!

"You did win, Mr. Scrumples," Kira agreed. "But come here! I don't think this fuzzball is just a fuzzball." She reached down and gently picked the fuzzball up. "This is a ... teenykin!"

Karina leaned over the side of the gazebo. "Why are you shouting, Kira?" she asked.

Queen Katia hurried over. "Is everything alright?" she asked, panting.

"It's a baby bunny!" Kira answered. She held the fuzzy teenykin out.

Karina scratched her head. "Why is there a baby bunny all alone out here?"

Kira shrugged. "Maybe she got lost. But she looks scared, doesn't she?" she asked. "I think Binky needs a home!"

Chapter 2

I guess you're naming her Binky,"
Queen Katia said.

Kira nodded and stroked Binky's
silky ears.

"She's very cute," Karina said.

"She's teenykin-tastic!" Kira agreed. "I think she's going to love it here with us."

Queen Katia raised an eyebrow. "You're not planning to keep Binky, are you?" she asked.

Kira gently placed Binky down on the ground. She whispered, "Make sure she doesn't get lonely, Mr. Scrumples." Then she said, "That was my plan."

Queen Katia sighed. "I know you love teenykins . . ." she began.

"I do!" Kira cried. Everyone in the Fruitdom knew that Kira had never met a teenykin she didn't love.

". . . but you have two pets now,"

Queen Katia continued, "and that's a lot of responsibility for one princess. Three would be too much."

Mom might be right, Kira thought. She was already taking care of Mr. Scrumples and her horse, Maisy. Then there were all the fruitizens' pets who sometimes needed an extra helping hand.

Kira glanced at Karina. "Do you want to adopt Binky?" she asked.

Karina lifted Binky up. She gave her a snuggle. But then she shook her head. "I'd love to, Kira. But I have to finish preparing for the Kiwi Jubilee," she said. She handed Binky back to Kira. "That's my responsibility right now."

"I think you need to take this teeny-kin to the Royal Animal Shelter," Queen Katia declared.

Kira looked at Binky. The bunny's nose twitched. Her eyes seemed to say *Please don't send me away.*

"I can't take her to the shelter!" Kira said. "Binky deserves a real home!"

"I'm sure a teenykin this adorable won't be in the shelter for long," Karina said. "Someone will adopt her soon."

But soon didn't feel like now. Kira frowned. "I know I can find Binky a real home," she said. "But how?"

"I believe in you," Queen Katia said. She patted Kira's shoulder. "I know you'll think of a way to find the right place for her."

Suddenly, Kira gasped. "I don't have to think of a way!" she exclaimed.

Queen Katia crossed her arms. "I already said Binky can't stay here. Please don't make me give a royal order."

"I know, Mom," Kira replied. "I just meant I don't have to think of the way all by myself. I can use Princess Power to help!"

"Well then," Queen Katia said, "here's a royal order to figure this problem out with some help from your friends!" She gave her daughter a big hug.

Kira touched the sparkly, kiwi-shaped charm on her friendship bracelet.

It beeped, and then a large purple kiwi bloomed in the sky! "The charm alarm will let my friends know that I need their help!" she announced. She waved goodbye to her family. "I have to get to the Punchbowl Treehouse!"

Chapter 3

Kira, Mr. Scrumples, and Binky hopped in Kira's motorboat and raced across the sea to Punchbowl Island.

Then they hurried up the ladder into the treehouse.

The other princesses hadn't arrived yet. But they were on their way! Kira saw something sparkle brightly on the shores of the Raspberry Fruitdom. It had to be one of Princess Rita's glimmering outfits! Rita zoomed toward Punchbowl Island in her bedazzled sailboat.

Then Kira saw two things in the sky. One was Princess Bea's glider from the Blueberry Fruitdom. The other was a plane from the Pineapple Fruitdom carrying Princess Penny and her cat, Fussy.

Bea jumped off the glider and whizzed along a zip line toward the treehouse.

Penny and Fussy waved as their parachute floated down.

Soon, all four friends were together again. Kira grinned. She held up the fuzzy baby bunny. "I'd like to introduce you to Binky! She was hiding in our garden, and she needs our help to find a home!"

"She's bedazzlous!" Rita said.

"Can I hold her, Kira?" Penny asked. "Please, please, please?"

"I want to hold her, too," Bea said, inching closer. She took Binky from Kira's hands and snuggled the bunny against her cheek. And then she sneezed! *"Achoo!"*

"Bless you!" Kira said.

"Do you need a tissue?" Rita asked. She reached into her sparkly bag and took out the most bedazzled sequined handkerchief Kira had ever seen!

Bea nodded. "Thank—*achoo!*" She sneezed again!

"Are you sick, Bea?" Rita asked.

"Do you have a cold?" Penny added, sounding worried.

Bea shook her head and said, "I haven't been sneezing at all today." Then she sneezed again!

Kira frowned. If Bea wasn't sick, why was she sneezing so much now? Suddenly, she had a guess. She took Binky from Bea and carried her to the other side of the treehouse. "Do you feel like sneezing now, Bea?" she asked.

Bea thought for a moment. "I don't think so," she said.

"Just what I thought," Kira said. "You have a bunny allergy!"

"How can I be allergic?" Bea asked. "I never sneeze around Fussy or Mr. Scrumples!"

"People can be allergic to bunnies even if they aren't allergic to cats or hamsters," Kira replied.

"A bunny allergy means," Penny said, "that Binky can't go home with Bea."

"So unfair!" Bea whined.

Kira turned to the others and said, "Rita? Penny? Do either of you want to adopt Binky?"

Rita shouted, "I do!" She ran to get to Binky. Her bracelets sparkled in the sunlight. But as she got near, Binky hopped away!

The jewels on her shoes sparkled as Rita stepped toward Binky again.

This time, Binky hopped back to Kira and hid behind her!

"Why does she keep running away from me?" Rita said.

"Maybe she's allergic to you?" Bea suggested, winking.

Then Kira realized why Binky was acting this way. It wasn't an allergy! "You're dazzling Binky!"

unnies are afraid of shiny or sparkly things," Kira explained.

"What?!" Rita gasped.

Penny said, "But Rita isn't even extra-glittery today."

"She's the same amount extra that she always is," Bea said.

Penny and Bea giggled. But Rita frowned. "This isn't even my most epic outfit," she said. "If this is scary to Binky, she really wouldn't like it in the Raspberry Kingdom."

"You do add a lot of sparkle," Penny said. "It's one of the things we love about you!"

"I guess I shouldn't adopt Binky either," Rita mumbled.

"That just leaves Penny," Kira said. "Do you think you want to adopt Binky?"

Penny scratched her head. "I don't know much about taking care of bunnies," she admitted.

"Don't worry," Kira replied. "I'm here to help you."

"So am I," added Rita.

"And so am I," added Bea. "Though I'll be helping from a distance."

"We'll work together to make sure Binky has the most teenykin-tastic home ever!" Kira said.

"Then there's only one thing left to do!" Penny exclaimed. "Pinkie-tea promise!"

Kira held her pinkie out. "We pinkie-tea promise to help those in need," she said.

Rita, Bea, and Penny extended their pinkies, too. "With our Princess Power, we'll always succeed!" they said

together. The pinkie-tea promise was complete!

"Most of the things that Binky will need are already in the Pineapple Palace," Kira said. "Healthy food, room to exercise, someone to snuggle."

"Check, check, and check!" Penny said.

Kira nodded. "There's one thing you'll need that you probably don't already have," she said. "A bunny hutch."

"What's that?" Bea asked. "And why does Binky need one?"

"Sometimes, bunnies need space to be by themselves," Kira explained.

Rita giggled. "Bunnies are a lot like princesses!" she joked.

Penny took a notebook out of her science kit. "Let's plan what the bunny hutch will look like," she said. Then she took out a ruler, a calculator, and three different colored pencils.

Bea winked and said, "We'd better get over there! If Penny takes out anything else, there won't be room for us!"

Penny grinned. "We want to do this right!"

"You can't argue with that, Bea!" Rita agreed.

"I'm just going to put Binky over there," Kira said, pointing to one of

Fussy's cat beds. "She can take a nap while we figure this out!"

Fussy had been lounging on a different cat bed. But as soon as Kira placed Binky down, Fussy got up and stretched. Then she padded across the room and climbed into the bed next to the bunny.

"Look!" Rita said. "Binky and Fussy are cuddling!"

"Maybe they can share while we work?" Bea suggested.

Fussy inched toward Binky, who looked like she would fall asleep right away. But then Mr. Scrumples started squeaking.

"Shh, Mr. Scrumples!" Kira said. "Let Binky sleep. You can join our planning meeting." But the hamster didn't budge.

"Leave him, Kira," Penny said. "We need your help over here."

Kira nodded. But then she heard a *hiss*. And a *plop*. She spun around toward the noise.

Fussy had scooted all the way to Binky's side of the bed. But they weren't snuggling. The *plop* was Binky being pushed off!

*B*ee stings! Kira thought. *Someone left the door open!*

As everyone watched, Binky hopped out of sight.

"Help!" Kira called. "Binky is running away!"

"That's not running," Bea said. "That's hopping."

"What difference does that make?" Rita asked. "This is a disaster of cotton-tail proportions!"

"Binky one, princesses zero," Bea added.

Kira raced to the open door. She looked right and left. "Which way did Binky go?"

Mr. Scrumples squeaked at Kira's feet. "What is it, Mr. Scrumples?" she asked. "Is it about Binky?"

The hamster nodded and pointed.

"Do you think she left the tree-house?" Penny asked.

Mr. Scrumples nodded again. Then he

hurried down the stairs. The girls trailed after him.

By the time they got outside, Kira was very worried. "Binky could be anywhere!" she moaned. "She's too little to take care of herself!"

"We'll find her, Kira," Bea said. "We'll work together!"

"Let's hop to it!" Penny added.

That's when Kira realized that Mr. Scrumples was missing, too. "Mr. Scrumples!" she cried. "Where are you?" She frowned. "How could I have lost two teenykins?"

"I see him!" Bea yelled. She grabbed Kira's hand. "Come on!"

Mr. Scrumples had stopped in front of a row of bushes. When the girls caught up to him, he pointed again.

"Is Binky hiding in there, Mr. Scrumples?" Kira asked. The hamster hopped up and down and nodded.

"It'll take forever to search under every branch and leaf!" Penny complained. "How are we ever going to find Binky?"

Mr. Scrumples ran to Bea's feet. Then he pretended to sneeze.

Bea shouted, "My allergies!"

"Are you feeling allergic again, Bea?" Kira asked. "Do you think you're allergic to other things outside, too?"

"I've never had a problem with

allergies before," Bea replied. "Not until I met Binky! But now it's lucky that I have a bunny allergy."

Mr. Scrumples grinned excitedly.

Kira's eyes grew wide. "I get it now! Since you'll sneeze if you get close to Binky, you can be our bunny detector!"

Chapter 6

The bunny search moved from bush to bush. Kira, Penny, and Rita kept their eyes out for any flashes of bunny fur. Bea took a big sniff at each bush.

"Not this one or this one or this one," Bea said. When she got to the fourth bush and sniffed, she opened her mouth to say something. But the only thing that came out was an *achoo!*

Rita and Penny high-fived. "Bunny detected!" Kira said, laughing.

"*Achoo!*" Bea sneezed again.

"Let's go back to the treehouse, Bea," Rita said. "Penny and Kira can get Binky. I don't want my glittery clothes to scare the bunny. And your nose has done enough!"

"We'll meet you back there in a flash!" Penny agreed.

Kira leaned down and pushed some leaves out of the way. She saw two silky ears poking out of a shallow hole. "There you are, Binky!"

Back in the Punchbowl Treehouse, everyone welcomed Binky back. "We'll keep a better eye on you from now on," Kira said. "Right, Mr. Scrumples?"

Mr. Scrumples nodded. He was ready to be a teenykin-tastic bunny bodyguard!

Across the room, Fussy stepped off her cat bed. "Even Fussy is happy to see Binky," Bea said. But before the cat came over, she grabbed some of her toys and dropped them on her bed. Then she grabbed a few more. When Fussy was done, there was no room for anything else—not even a baby bunny.

The message was clear. "We can officially say Fussy isn't ready for a pet-mate," Penny said. "So I don't think I can adopt Binky after all." She looked down at the floor. "I'm sorry, Kira. I really wanted to help."

Kira smiled. "I know you did, Penny," she said. "But your first responsibility is to take care of Fussy. And you can't bring something—or someone—who would make Fussy uncomfortable into your home. It wouldn't be fair."

"So what do we do now?" Bea asked from across the room.

Kira gulped. It was almost time for the Kiwi Jubilee. She had to get Binky settled quickly. "I think I'm going to have to bring Binky to the Royal Animal Shelter, like my mom told me to," she answered.

"We'll go with you," Rita said. She put her hand on Kira's shoulder. "We'll go together and *still* find Binky a home."

I just need to figure out where that home will be! Kira thought.

$\mathcal{T}$he Royal Animal Shelter was a small building across from the Kiwi Palace. It was very cozy—and very noisy! There were a lot of teenykins inside waiting for homes. Kira counted three puppies, two kittens, a pot-bellied pig, a snake, two iguanas, and even a peacock!

"Look at them!" Rita said. "They're all so adorablicious!"

"I want to take some home with me!" Bea added. "As long as I'm not allergic."

"Binky is the cutest one, though," Penny said. "I'm sure she'll find a home first."

Kira frowned. Binky was cute. But all the teenykins were cute! They all deserved homes.

That's when Kira thought of something. She turned to Rita. "Can I borrow a crayon?"

Rita looked through her art kit and

found one. "Why do you need it?" she asked.

Kira walked up to a poster for the party. She scribbled on it. When she stepped back, her friends read the new words.

"You are brilliant, Kira!" Bea said.

"The Kiwi Jubilee is just the place to find homes for all these animals!" Penny added.

"But there's so much to do if we're going to have all the teenykins ready for tonight," Kira said. "So I need everyone's princess help again!"

The girls high-fived each other. Then Kira asked, "Where do we start?"

"With a spectaculacious makeover, of course!" Rita declared. "I'll take care of that."

"The animals have to be squeaky-clean first," Bea said. "I'm still allergic to bunnies. But I can take everyone else for a bath."

"I'll bathe Binky," Penny offered. "But where are you going to find a tub big enough for three puppies, two kittens, a pot-bellied pig, a snake, two iguanas, and a peacock?"

Bea was always ready to roll up her sleeves and dive into a problem. She said, "Who needs a tub when we have the sea?"

"Perfect!" Kira agreed.

Bea turned to the teenykins. "I think we should race to the water," she said, giggling. "Last one there's a rotten egg!"

Before Bea and the teenykins made their exit, Rita added, "I'll start on outfits while you're taking them for a dip."

"It won't matter how clean or sparkly the animals are if our fruitizens don't know about the adoptions," Kira said, frowning. "We already sent invitations out. And we didn't mention any teeny-kin adoptions."

"Skywriting can fix that!" Penny ex-claimed. "After the bunny bath, I can fly in my plane and put the invitation somewhere everyone can see it."

Kira laughed. "What are we waiting for?"

hile Bea splashed and Rita bedazzled, Penny and Fussy hopped in
her plane. They wrote a huge announce-
ment in the sky: NEW TONIGHT, BY ROYAL
DECREE, THE KIWI ADOPTION JUBILEE!

But there was still something that needed to be done. Kira hugged a freshly bathed Binky and said, "Today, I learned that giving an animal a good home is about more than thinking it's adorable. You must know what a teenykin really needs to properly care for one."

Kira winked at her hamster. "Right, Mr. Scrumples?" He nodded and nuzzled closer to Kira.

"I'm going to write out some information about each of the teenykins here," Kira continued. "That way, fruitizens can decide if they can give a teenykin a good home. I'll call them . . . fur-sonality cards! What do you think, Mr. Scrumples?"

Mr. Scrumples grinned.

"I'm glad you agree," Kira said. She gave Binky's soft ears a good scratch. "And I think I'll start with this one!"

Queen Katia wasn't surprised to see Kira returning to the Kiwi Palace with her three best friends. She wasn't even surprised that Kira still had Binky with her. What made Queen Katia speechless was when Kira returned with Penny, Rita, Bea, Mr. Scrumples, Fussy, Binky, *and* three puppies, two kittens, a pot-bellied pig, a snake, two iguanas, and a peacock!

"Kira!" Queen Katia shouted. "I told you to bring Binky to the Royal Animal

Shelter. You weren't supposed to bring the whole shelter back here!"

"We were trying to find a home for Binky," Kira explained. "But then we realized that *all* these teenykins deserve homes!"

Queen Katia put her hands on her hips. "You can't have thirteen pets, Kira! That's way, way, way too many!"

"Don't worry, Mom," Kira replied. "We have a plan."

Just then, her sister, Karina, ran up. "Did you see the message in the sky?" she asked, panting and pointing.

"I wrote that!" Penny exclaimed. "It's pineapple perfection!"

Queen Katia looked up at the sky-writing. She scrunched her brows. "The Kiwi *Adoption* Jubilee?"

"That's our plan!" Kira said. "The Kiwi Jubilee celebrates Kiwi kindness. What is kinder than giving a teenykin a home?"

"We thought the guests could meet the animals and learn about them," Penny said.

"And fall in love with how adorablicious they are," Rita said.

"And maybe adopt one," Bea added. "As long as they don't have an allergy."

"What a great idea," Karina said. She patted Binky's head. "I think they might all find new homes tonight."

Queen Katia said, "I have another royal order. I want us all to do our best to find these pets wonderful new homes!"

"Then let's get this party started!" Kira declared.

Chapter 9

Fruitizens from all four Fruitdoms arrived at the Kiwi Palace. They were happy to see each other and celebrate their acts of kindness. But they were even more delighted to see all the animals!

"You really got them all squeaky-clean, Bea," Kira whispered. "Even the pot-bellied pig!"

"Bea one, dirt zero!" Bea said, winking.

"And those outfits are fantabulous, Rita," Kira added.

Rita smiled. "They are, aren't they?" she said.

"Where did you find so many teenykin-sized tiaras?" Penny asked.

"I'm always prepared!" Rita replied.

Almost immediately, the teenykins were finding homes. When they did, Kira made sure that every new pet family was given the correct fur-sonality card. "This will tell you everything you need to know to take good care of your teenykin!" she said.

Penny's brother, Felipe, was very excited to be taking the snake home. Queen Ryung of the Raspberry Fruitdom decided the peacock would be a lovely addition to their palace. "This peacock is almost as extra as you are, Rita!" she told her daughter, grinning.

"What can I say?" Rita replied, shrugging. "We both have Rita-rrific style!"

Kira caught one of Bea's fathers, Sir Benedict, sharing a peanut butter sandwich with the pot-bellied pig. "Look, Kira!" he called. "I've made a new friend."

Kira giggled. "Well, pot-bellied pigs love peanut butter. I'm not surprised you two are getting along!"

"We really are," Sir Benedict replied. "In fact, this little guy should come back to the Blueberry Fruitdom with me."

"Then you'll need this!" Kira said. She handed the pig's fur-sonality card to Sir Benedict.

Next, Kira noticed Penny's Great Aunt Busyboots. She had a kitten in each hand. She looked like she'd absolutely fallen in love. "We are taking you two back to the Pineapple Palace, aren't we?" she crooned.

"I'm not sure Fussy is ready for a pet-mate," Penny said.

Fussy nodded—until Busyboots gave her a look. "Fussy can learn to share," she said.

"You're right," Kira said. "Cats *can* learn to share their space. But you need to give Fussy time to get used to the new kittens." She held out the fur-sonality cards for the kittens. "There are more tips here on making these tee-nykins feel at home."

Busyboots placed the kittens on the ground next to her long skirt. The kittens scurried to hide under the fabric. "Don't worry. No one will force them together. They can stay right here with me until all three cats are ready to get along."

Fussy meowed at Busyboots's skirt. The kittens stayed hidden. But then Fussy did something surprising. She popped under the skirt, too. "Should we be worried?" Penny asked.

Before Kira answered, Fussy popped out again. This time, the kittens followed her. "They might be getting along," Kira whispered. "But knowing Fussy, you should go check, just in case!"

Chapter 10

*A*lmost all the teenykins have found homes! Kira thought, smiling.

She only had one fur-sonality card left. It was Binky's! *Why hasn't Binky found a home?* she wondered. She looked around to see if anyone was playing with the baby bunny.

Kira saw Bea helping Sir Benedict give their pig another peanut butter sandwich. She spotted Rita drape a sparkly scarf around her peacock. She saw Penny sitting with Fussy and the kittens. All three cats were now wearing matching jeweled collars and identical tiaras. But she couldn't see Binky anywhere!

I don't know what to do! Kira thought. She frowned. That's when she heard someone ask, "Is something wrong?" It was Queen Katia. "You look upset."

Kira gulped. "I think Binky has run away again!" she exclaimed. "What if something happened? What if she got scared?"

"Kira," Queen Katia said. She took her daughter's hands. "Come with me."

"But, Mom," Kira moaned, "I have to look for Binky!"

Queen Katia didn't listen. She led Kira around the corner. Suddenly, Kira saw Karina—with Binky!

"What are you doing with Binky, Karina?" Kira asked.

Karina scooped Binky up. "I was thinking about adopting her." She grinned. "Do you think she'd be happy here with us?"

Kira's mouth dropped open. "But Mom said no to another teenykin!"

Queen Katia laughed. "I said *you* couldn't take care of a third pet," she said. "But Karina doesn't have any pets yet. She can take the responsibility of a baby bunny."

"But I won't be able to do it alone," Karina added, winking. "Will you help me, Kira?"

"Of course I will!" Kira agreed. She handed Binky's fur-sonality card to her sister. "Don't worry if you don't learn everything on this card. I'll be here to remind you!"

The girls giggled.

"I'm really proud of you, Kira," Queen Katia said. She put her arm around Kira's shoulders. "You made sure every teenykin here has somewhere to call home. That is true Kiwi kindness. And *that's* what being a princess is all about: helping others."

Kira knew that she couldn't have done it without her friends. Together, there was no challenge they couldn't face! She smiled and replied, "Princess Power saved the day!"

Read more fruit-tastic adventures...

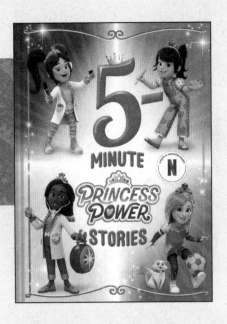

...and don't miss:

Now on Netflix!

About the Author

Sudipta Bardhan-Quallen is an award-winning author whose work includes *Roxie Loves Adventure, Tyrannosaurus Wrecks!*, the Purrmaids chapter book series, and over sixty more books. A princess at heart, she enjoys dressing up and being pampered—but she's always up for tackling problems and getting her hands dirty. Sudipta lives in New Jersey with her husband, three kids, and an adorable pug named Roxie. Find out more about her and her books by visiting sudipta.com.